Praise for

THE **CREATURE** FROM MY **CLOSET** SERIES

"Original and hilarious." —*School Library Journal*

"Highly amusing new series starter. . . . Skye gives Rob a self-deprecating charm and highlights the pleasures of books both subtly and effectively."
—*Booklist*

"This pitch-perfect offering should appeal to reluctant readers, not to mention the legion Wimpy Kid fans."
—*Shelf Awareness*

"Rob's dry commentary on his family, school, and social life is sure to provoke laughs."
—*Publishers Weekly*

THE LORD OF THE HAT

THE CREATURE
FROM MY
CLOSET

written and illustrated by

OBERT SKYE

Christy Ottaviano Books

Henry Holt and Company ✦ New York

Henry Holt and Company, LLC
Publishers since 1866
175 Fifth Avenue
New York, New York 10010
mackids.com

Henry Holt® is a registered trademark of Henry Holt and Company, LLC.
Text copyright © 2015 by Obert Skye
Illustrations copyright © 2015 by Obert Skye

Library of Congress Cataloging-in-Publication Data
Skye, Obert.
Lord of the Hat / Obert Skye.—First edition.
    pages cm.—(The creature from my closet ; book 5)
Summary: "Rob Burnside is visited by an especially strange closet creature: the
CAT IN THE HAT mashed with GOLLUM from The Lord of the Rings"—Provided by publisher.
ISBN 978-1-62779-162-5 (hardback) — ISBN 978-1-62779-550-0 (e-book)
[1. Monsters—Fiction. 2. Books and reading—Fiction. 3. Humorous stories.] I. Title.
PZ7.S62877Lo2015   [Fic]—dc23   2015008295

Our books may be purchased in bulk for promotional, educational, or business use. Please
contact your local bookseller or the Macmillan Corporate and Premium Sales Department at
(800) 221-7945 ext. 5442 or by e-mail at MacmillanSpecialMarkets@macmillan.com.

First Edition—2015
Designed by Eileen Savage
Printed in the United States of America by
R. R. Donnelley & Sons Company, Harrisonburg, Virginia

1 3 5 7 9 10 8 6 4 2

To Christy Ottaviano—
One Amazing Editor, Person, and Friend

CONTENTS

CHAPTER 1

~

CALM BEFORE THE STORM

In a house on the ground there lives a Robert.
That's me. Robert Columbo Burnside. My family also
lives in that same house. Their names are coming in
a moment. Families are kind of weird. I mean, I like
mine, but it's sort of strange that we all have to get
along and live together under one roof.

These days there are all kinds of families. I saw a show about a man with a parrot and a coatrack who kept talking about them all being family.

There's a TV station that always features Today's New Family. But then all they show are programs about people who live in swamps and movies about superheroes or witches.

Yep, families come in all shapes and sizes. I guess if I had to describe my family, I would say it's medium-sized and kind of boring. My mom naps a lot on the couch, my dad thinks things like jigsaw puzzles are exciting, my older sister, Libby, spends a good part of her day looking in the mirror, and my little brother, Tuffin, is crazy about a terrible kid show called *Toe Time*.

My family is pretty bland. Normal things like family dinners are usually a snoozefest at my house. We don't always eat together, but when we do, sometimes it puts me to sleep. If anyone ever made a movie or TV show out of one of our normal dinners, it would be pretty dull and the cast would be kind of lame.

FAMILY DINNER

STARRING
ROB BURNSIDE

DID SOMEONE SAY AVERAGE?

FEATURING
DAD AND MOM

RAISE THE CEILING!

EARL

KAREN

I'D LIKE TO TAKE A NAP FIRST.

UNFORTUNATELY FEATURING
LIBBY

HEY, WAIT, I SHOULD BE THE STAR.

ALSO STARRING
TUFFIN

WATCH ME NOT BLINK.

WITH SPECIAL GUEST APPEARANCES FROM
PUCK and FRED

- ARF
ARF

BRAAAAAAK

TONIGHT'S EPISODE:
THE DRY CHICKEN

It might *be* a stretch comparing my family to a movie, *but* I have movies on my mind. Sure, my closet has *been* pushing *books* on me, but this week my brain's thinking about movies.

I like previews for movies, I like movie theaters, and I even like watching movies on TV. But what really has me pumped about movies is making them. Last week my *best* friend, Trevor, got a video camera from his dad. Since then we've been filming things with our other friends in our spare time. Then we upload the movies to YouTube. We've only finished one movie, but already it has thirty-seven views.

Everyone has been making suggestions about what our second movie should be. Some suggestions are way better than others.

We appreciate the ideas, but Trevor and I already know what our next big movie will be. It's based on a script that I wrote. It's called *Mustache and the Mighty Cool Adventure.* I'm going to play the star, Mustache, but we're going to use our other friends to help.

So I've been thinking about Mustache and making movies. I've also been thinking about Janae. She lives right next to my house, and ever since she kissed me at the Fun-ger Games Funstival, we seem to be getting along great. Plus, Maggie, who is a girl that lives four houses down, told Teddy some good news:

Maggie said Janae was sure, which was pretty amazing. A while ago Janae was so mad at me I didn't think she'd ever speak to me again. But that was then, and this is now. Besides, the reason she was mad at me had more to do with my closet than anything else. It's not a normal place to hang clothes and store shoes. If you're already aware of what my closet can do, then you're welcome to close your eyes for the next few lines.

When I was a little kid, I had a walk-in closet with no closet door that I wanted to turn into a science lab. I collected things like salad dressing and nail polish and glue and whatever I could find that was a sticky liquid. I took all those things and mixed them together in my closet in an attempt to make stuff. I never really created anything great.

At some point, I stopped trying to create things and just used my closet to store all the books that my mom forced on me. She used to have a job at a bookstore and brought books home all the time. It really wasn't fair. It's one thing for parents to talk about books, but it's another thing when parents have access to so many. Sometimes I felt buried in the books she brought home.

My mom would also bring books home for my brother, Tuffin, but his were all picture books and super easy to read.

Too many books! That's why I threw all of mine into the closet, along with goop and the mess from my fake lab. When my closet really began to change, however, was when my dad brought home an odd closet door he found at a garage sale. The door was heavy and old. It also had an embarrassing sticker on it that we couldn't peel off and a really weird doorknob. The doorknob was made of brass, and it had a little bearded man on the front. I named him Beardy.

A few months back, my room got so messy I couldn't move around in it.

My mom made me clean everything up. I shoved
most of it into my closet. Then I shut the door and
figured that was that. But that wasn't that, that
was this, and this is my life where I now have a
closet that mixes the books and supplies together.
It also brings strange creatures to life, mash-ups
that I have to deal with and figure out why they are
here. The first creature that came out of my closet
was Wonkenstein. He was more than a handful. He
was sort of a foot-full.

Then there was the Potterwookiee, also known as Hairy, who made me hang out in cemeteries and fly in vans and cook things I didn't know how to cook.

The third creature was Pinocula, and he filled my life with confusion and lies.

And the last thing to emerge from my closet was Katfish. She was also the best thing. Not only was she kind, but she helped fix things at Softrock Middle School, where I had messed stuff up.

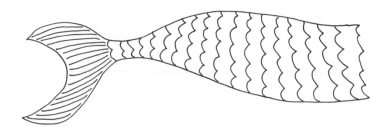

I like that my life is calm now. It's nice to catch my breath and not worry about any messes for a while. My closet's locked, my friends are behaving, and my mom isn't mad at me. I'd say that's something to celebrate. And in my house when we celebrate, it usually involves Tuffin throwing food.

PEA PARTY!

I GUESS THIS IS BETTER THAN YOUR SOUP CELEBRATIONS.

CHAPTER 2

THE ANNOUNCEMENT

Actually, the dinner we were having was nothing to celebrate, unless they were giving out trophies for boring meals.

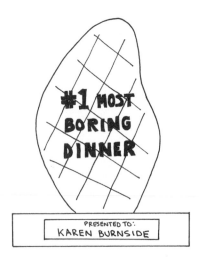

#1 MOST BORING DINNER

PRESENTED TO:
KAREN BURNSIDE

I mean, I like my life calm, but not my food. We were having more chicken and some sort of salad and peas. My mom always served peas even though none of us liked them. Tuffin just threw his, Libby hid hers in her napkin, and I always slipped mine up onto one of the hidden slats under the table. My dad wasn't home from work yet, which was unusual. Normally he came home early and watched TV or helped us do our homework. We were just about to worry when he pulled up to the house and honked twice like he always did.

A couple of seconds later, he came busting through the door. He was smiling and singing some song about good fortune.

He patted me on the head, pinched Tuffin on the cheek, and winked at Libby. He then picked up my mom and kissed her. It sort of made me lose my appetite.

It wasn't unusual for my dad to be happy. He was a smiling, double-honking, complimenting, loud-laughing kind of guy. Everyone was his friend, and the world was a place he liked. He loved his job, he loved wearing a suit and tie every day, and he loved, well . . . he loved everything.

He was embarrassing like all dads, but at least he was nice. Rourk's dad was embarrassing and the opposite of nice.

So we were all pretty interested in what was making our dad act *so* happy. He was practically bouncing off the walls, and there were at least ten things out of place on him.

I had no idea what the great news was. I was aware, though, that my dad and me had very different opinions about what was great. He thought things like ant farms and self-discipline were fantastic, while I thought things like the latest video games and pools shaped like money signs were more "da bomb." So I was pretty sure that whatever my dad was hopped up about would be something I didn't care for. My dad kept singing and dancing around the table until my mom gently said,

TELL US THE GOOD NEWS RIGHT NOW!

Okay, you need to know this. My dad has his own business. It's called Earl M. Burnside and Associates. He sells playgrounds and basketball courts and really anything that you might find at a playground or gym. Well, according to my dad, his company had just won the award for . . .

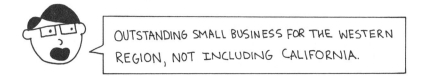

OUTSTANDING SMALL BUSINESS FOR THE WESTERN REGION, NOT INCLUDING CALIFORNIA.

We all congratulated him and then went back to eating our chicken. I'm glad I didn't get too excited. I was happy for my dad, but the award didn't sound very impressive. I mean, who wants to win for the smallest business? My dad did like little things, so I could see why he was pumped up. He liked little snacks, little puzzles, little stories. He even liked little cheap headphones, where I liked the big ones.

I'M PRETENDING THE SOUND IS GOOD.

I CAN'T HEAR YOU.

My dad continued to jump up and down. I
guessed he had more good news to tell us. Since he
had won for being the outstanding small business
for the western region, not including California, he
had also won a trip for eight to a fancy hotel in
New Mexico.

Libby started to huff and puff about what I had
said until my mom spoke up:

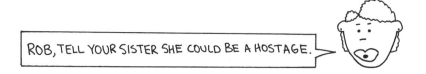

My dad went on and on about how he had
already rented an RV and we were going to leave
this Sunday and drive to New Mexico and stop at
interesting sights.

We were also going to take a famous old mountain
train to a beautiful hotel where he was going to be
the honored guest at a banquet where he would get
his award for being the . . .

OUTSTANDING SMALL BUSINESS FOR THE WESTERN REGION, NOT INCLUDING CALIFORNIA.

I was a little excited. If we were going next week, that meant I would be able to miss some school. Besides, I had never been to New Mexico. It could be fun. I mean, it might be nice to take a trip and get away from it all.

 I HAVEN'T TOLD YOU THE BEST NEWS YET.

Uh-oh. My stomach started to hurt, and I could actually see fear in my sister's eyes. The last time we had heard my dad mention "best news yet" was when he had signed us up as a family to sing a song in church.

It turned out that the *best* news this time was almost as bad. Since the trip was for eight people and we only had five, my dad had invited my uncle and aunt and their obnoxious son, Kyle.

Libby started to cry and ran off. My mom looked upset, and Tuffin started to chant.

This was not good. Even though Tuffin liked him, Kyle was the worst. I was amazed at how much I now missed our normal boring dinners.

CHAPTER 3

~

NOTES

All right, I should talk a bit more about my closet. After all, it is the reason for me keeping these notes and drawing these pictures. I do it for science. It's so I'll have documented proof of what has been happening. I think the world deserves to know. My closet used to have no character. Now it has piles of character. Just keep reading and turning the pages. You'll see what I mean.

This is my closet:

This is my closet on books:

My closet has been locked up tight since Katfish splashed back into it. Kat had said that things were going to get weirder, but so far Beardy is keeping the door locked. It's been over two weeks, and I haven't heard any noises or seen any sign that the closet is about to open. I've actually tried to get Beardy to unlock the door and let me look inside. But Beardy's not budging; he's as stubborn as always.

Not only would I like to get into my closet for the creatures' sake, but I would also like to take out some of the things that I put in there. I know my favorite basketball is inside and a couple of my Thumb Buddies. I'm missing at least three that I know of.

MINETACK   MIDDLE-AGED   MY
             MUTATED NINJA   LITTLE
             TORTOISE   DONKEY

After dinner I went to my room to do my homework. I could still hear my dad talking enthusiastically in the family room about the trip and renting an RV. I was trying to be happy for him, but traveling with Kyle was not a pretty thought.

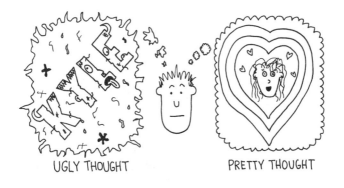

UGLY THOUGHT   PRETTY THOUGHT

Every once in a while when my aunt goes to play bingo, I have to babysit him. And the last time I babysat, he burned some of my leg hairs off with his mom's curling iron that he was pretending was a lightsaber.

OUCH!

THE FORCE SMELLS LIKE BURNT GARBAGE.

He was even worse when he was with Tuffin. Tuffin did everything Kyle did. He wanted to wear what Kyle was wearing, talk like Kyle, and act exactly like him. Now the two of them were going to be trapped in our RV as we drove for hours. I really needed a reason not to go on the trip.

After I finished my homework, a really strange urge washed over me. I can't explain it exactly, but for some reason, I felt like I wanted to write Janae a note. Sure, things had been so much better these last two weeks, but I didn't think our relationship was ready for notes. That was a pretty serious step. Still, I couldn't fight the urge to scribble out a few words and deliver them to Janae. I was planning to head to the island to work on filming *Mustache and the Mighty Cool Adventure* with my friends, but my brain was ruining things by telling me to write a note. . . .

I got out a pencil and a piece of paper—that part didn't feel weird. I have been doing a lot of writing lately. I wouldn't call myself a writer, but I've been writing these books, writing little movie scripts, and doing a lot of writing in my homework.

IF YOU ARE ALWAYS SCRIBBLING THINGS ON PAPER... YOU MIGHT BE A WRITER.

Now I was writing a note to Janae. Creating the note was easy. The words just seemed to come to me. My hand flew over the paper as my mind clicked and whirred. I almost wasn't sure what I was writing. But after a few moments, my hand stopped and I looked down at my paper in surprise.

```
I AM ROB
ROB I AM.
YOU'RE JANAE
YES SIR MA'AM.
WE ARE NEIGHBORS
YOU AND I.
YOU'RE A GIRL
AND I'M A GUY.
WE SHOULD HANG OUT
YES WE SHOULD.
AT THE MALL
TOMORROW'S GOOD.
WE COULD TALK
OR EAT SOME FOOD.
I WON'T BURP
OR BE RUDE.
YOU'LL SEE THAT I'M
AN OKAY DUDE
WITH A SUPER ATTITUDE!
```

I couldn't believe it. Not only had I written a note for Janae, I had written it in a rhyme. And not a very good rhyme. I didn't feel like myself.

SOMETHINGS WRONG WITH ME.

I wondered if this was how the great poets of the world got started. One day they woke up and felt compelled to send notes to the person they liked.

My thinking was interrupted by my best friend knocking on my window. Of all the people I hung out with, Trevor was my closest friend. He might have crooked glasses and weak basketball skills, but he was cool, and not quite as much trouble as my other friends.

My friends used my bedroom window instead of our front door. It didn't make my mom happy, but it made things easier for us. It was like my own private entrance.

Trevor crawled through the window and into my room. He was excited and talkative as usual.

More than anything, I wanted to go out and work on the movie, but I was still a little worried about the note I had written and the feelings I had for Janae. I knew Trevor might laugh at me, but I had nobody else to talk to. I needed to brainstorm about what I should do with the note and figure out why I had written it. So I pulled it out of my pocket and gave it to him to read.

I told Trevor how I had felt like I had to write it, and he told me how he felt like he had to floss at least three times a day or else his gums would swell and bleed. I then told him to not tell me things like that, and he told me . . .

FRIENDSHIP IS ABOUT COMMUNICATION.

I tried to communicate that I knew what I had written wasn't very good, but there was still a little bit of me that wanted to give the note to Janae. I figured she would think it was funny. She had liked the poem I wrote with Wonkenstein. She had also liked the song that Katfish had written and that she thought I sang. Actually, that song was what had caused Janae to forgive and kiss me. Heck, if those

lame things had impressed Janae, this poem might
get her to go on a date with me.

Trevor was right. As a normal middle school
student, I was appropriately awkward. But when I
added my closet to my life, I was poem-writing,
cooking-contest, dance-ruining, girl-singing kind of
weird.

I walked over and looked Beardy straight in the eyes. He didn't blink. I grabbed him and tried for the thousandth time to pull him open. Trevor reached out and pulled with me. When that didn't work, both of us took turns kicking. Still the closet door stayed locked. Trevor stopped kicking and asked,

I figured he wanted to dry himself off from the sweating the kicking had caused, but he had another reason. He had seen a show on TV about how some crooks had broken out of a locked room

by heating the doorknob with a blow-dryer until the lock got so hot it clicked open.

It was worth a shot. I ran to the bathroom and got Libby's blow-dryer. It was a really expensive one that she had warned me never to touch. I knew that if she understood how important this was she would ... still not let me use it. So I didn't ask. I brought the blow-dryer back to my room and plugged it in. I was worried that Libby might hear the blow-dryer, so I turned on my radio really loud.

Trevor leaned down and put his ear by the knob to listen for it unlocking. I should have closed my window because Jack was out on the island and he heard the noise and came to investigate. I think he was confused by what he found.

I don't know what song was on the radio, but it was awful. Jack climbed through the window acting like everything was normal. I turned off the blow-dryer and told him that we were trying to get into the closet. Before I could say anything else, he reached out and grabbed the now-hot Beardy.

It was a good thing that the music was loud, because Jack's screaming was pretty bad. As soon as he calmed down, I rushed him to the bathroom, where we ran his hand under cold water. I knew it hurt, but Jack was trying to act like it was no big deal.

After running his hand under the water for ten minutes, he dried it off and we went back to my room. Trevor was still blow-drying Beardy, but it hadn't done anything except fluff Beardy's hair.

Trevor turned off the blow-dryer, and I turned off the music. Trevor looked around for something he could use to open the hot doorknob. He spotted Hairy's scarf on my dresser and grabbed it. Using the scarf like a hot pad, he tried to open the door, but there was still no budge.

Jack was whining about his hand so I asked to see it. He turned it over, and we all gasped.

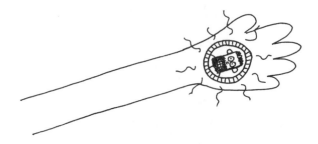

I think only Beardy was happy about what we saw. Jack had a perfect imprint of my closet doorknob on his palm. It was the reverse image of Beardy. It looked painful but also kind of cool.

Jack was interrupted by Libby coming through my door. She was not happy about me using the blow-dryer.

My friends left, and I spent the next couple minutes promising my mom and Libby I would never touch Libby's stuff again. If our house had been an old-fashioned school, I would have run out of chalk writing down my apology.

CHAPTER 4

MISSING

In the morning when I got up, I noticed that the top of my dresser looked wrong. It usually looked like this:

WONKENSTEIN'S CANE

HAIRY'S SCARF

KATFISH'S BOW & ARROWS

Today it looked like this:

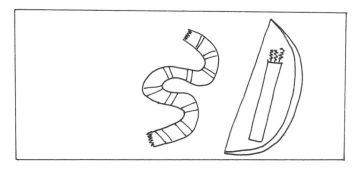

Even if you are horrible at guessing games, you should be able to easily guess what was missing. If not, I can make it easier. Pretend I'm a children's cartoon, and you yell what's missing at the TV screen.

The small cane that Wonkenstein had left me was no longer there, and I had a pretty good idea who might have taken it.

Libby probably took the cane to get even. Well, I needed it back. I had been given something from all four of my creature visitors, and all of them had told me to take care of the gifts because I would need them in the future. Jim, the bat/cricket that had stayed with me after Pinocula left, wasn't on my dresser, but he was somewhere in my neighborhood. Wonk's cane was way more important than Libby's dumb blow-dryer. She could buy another one. Wonk's cane was one of a kind. I ran to her room and confronted her.

I DIDN'T TAKE ANYTHING OF YOURS, BECAUSE EVERYTHING YOU OWN IS DISGUSTING.

I could usually tell when she was lying, because she would close her eyes. Well, her eyes were wide open and she seemed honestly surprised by what I was asking. So I went to accuse Tuffin, but he was still sleeping so he probably didn't take it. When I asked my mom, she said the same thing she always says whenever we misplace something:

MAYBE IT WAS THROWN OUT.

My mom wasn't being mean. She just had three kids, and she didn't have the energy to look for every LEGO and homework assignment we might have lost under the couch.

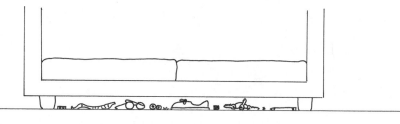

I went back to my room and checked to see if
the cane had fallen behind my dresser. It hadn't. I
looked on my desk and under my beanbag. It wasn't
there or there. I looked in my dresser drawers and
under the blankets on my bed. No cane. I got down
on my knees and looked under my bed.

Nothing. I did find one of Tuffin's shirts. That
wasn't too surprising, seeing how Tuffin left his
stuff everywhere. I pulled the shirt out and . . .

There was cat hair all over it. I had no idea what cat Tuffin had been playing with, but it sure shed a lot.

I was worried about Wonk's cane, but I needed to get ready for school. So I pushed those thoughts aside and took a shower. While eating breakfast, I asked my dad about the cane.

After breakfast I rode the bus to school. It's strange how different going to school is ever since

Katfish left. People don't hate me and nobody gives me grief. Unless you're talking about Chris Heck, who has supercool hair and gives everybody grief about how uncool theirs is.

I brought the note I had written for Janae with me to school. I couldn't decide what to do with it. I had been arguing with myself all morning about it.

By lunchtime I was so worked up about it that I could barely eat. Trevor thought I should just be a man and throw the note away. I was considering doing that when Jack came up to our table to show us his hand. The imprint of Beardy was still there. Jack was pretty proud of it. He was showing everyone and telling them that it was the symbol of a bearded street gang. I didn't blame him; telling people it was my closet doorknob didn't sound quite as cool. Jack said that he was even thinking of getting his brother to make some T-shirts of Beardy to . . .

COMPLETE MY LOOK.

I hadn't noticed, but while Jack had been talking to me and Trevor, I had been scribbling something

on my napkin with my pen. When Jack walked off to
show some other people his palm, I looked down
and gasped.

ONE
KISS
TWO
KISS
JANAE
KISS
YOU
KISS

What was wrong with me? I covered the napkin
so no one would see. Trevor could tell something was
up by the way I was hunched over. He asked me if I
was okay, and I sheepishly showed him the napkin.

Trevor pointed out that I was acting like a nut. He also pointed out that what I had just written was very Dr. Seuss-ish.

MAYBE DR. SEUSS IS IN YOUR CLOSET.

GOOD. I THINK I NEED A DOCTOR.

HE'S NOT A REAL DOCTOR.

TOO BAD, BECAUSE I'M REAL SICK.

I didn't finish my lunch. I didn't even finish the conversation. I got up and walked across the cafeteria, wadded up the napkin, and threw it into the trash. Then I walked down the hall to put my lunch in my locker. I noticed Janae's locker number: 384. I stopped and stared at it.

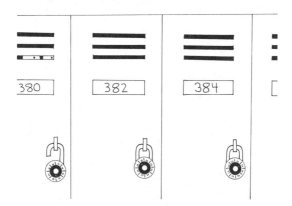

380   382   384   [

Nobody besides me was in the hall. I had thrown the napkin away, but I still had the rhyming note I had written yesterday. It felt like it was burning a hole in my back pocket.

I knew I could easily put the note into her locker without anyone seeing. Janae might like it. She might also think I'm a rhyming stalker.

I stopped thinking and just did it. Something must really have been wrong with me. I had a good thing going with Janae, and now I had just willingly made it weird. I stepped back from the locker and sighed. Teddy saw me and said,

I ignored Teddy and walked down the hall alone. It was very possible I had just made a huge mistake. Who gives a rhyming note to a girl? I suddenly felt very alone and extra dorky.

CHAPTER 5

MUSTARD BURGER

I like most surprises, but there are some I could live without. For example, I don't like finding Libby's long hair in my cereal.

But I do enjoy good surprises, like when I get a check from my grandpa for being...

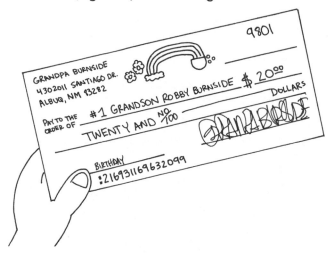

Or when my parents go shopping at one of those big warehouse grocery club stores and come home with *boxes* of food that we usually never buy.

But even the good surprises don't compare to the great surprise I got after school when I was walking down the hall with Trevor. Maggie, Janae's friend, stopped me and said,

Maggie walked off, and I looked at Trevor. He seemed even more surprised than me. In fact, he was so shocked that his glasses were straight for once.

I couldn't believe the note I slipped into Janae's locker had worked. In the history of notes, it was one of the dumbest.

I didn't have time to think about how lucky I was. I needed to get home and get my homework done so I could slip out my window and get to the mall by four. Plus, I needed to spend at least fifteen minutes brushing my teeth to get my breath in good shape.

I SMELL BUFF.

I was lucky. When I got home, my mom was taking a nap on the couch and Tuffin was at a neighbor's house playing. I did my homework in record time and then brushed

my teeth and combed my hair in a way that made it look like I wasn't a baby. I also put on a little body spray. While slipping out my window, I was greeted by another surprise. This one seemed to shock me almost as much as Janae liking my note.

It was Jim. The preachy half-bat, half-cricket that had come out of the closet with Pinocula and

never gone back in. Despite him *being a little bossy*,
I was happy to *see* him.

I didn't like the *sound* of that. I bet nobody has
ever been happy to *see* trouble show up at their
party.

Jim flew into my room and rested on my dresser,
where Wonk's cane used to be. He took off his tiny

top hat and dusted the brim of it. He then put it back on and cleared his throat.

I explained to Jim that I was wearing body spray because I was going to meet someone at the mall, and that it was important that I smelled good because . . .

It was a lie, of course. I was wearing body spray because of Janae. But the mall still does smell like feet. Since Jim had come with Pinocula, he knew all about lying, so he didn't buy the one I was telling. He told me that he had been hanging around and knew all about my plan to meet Janae.

I ALSO KNOW SOMETHING IMPORTANT. SOMETHING VERY IMPORTANT. YOU NEED TO KNOW THAT—

Jim was interrupted by the sound of something hitting my window. I looked over and saw an egg running down the pane.

I looked out my window, and what did I see? Nothing. If one of my friends had thrown the egg, he would still have been there laughing and pointing at me. It wasn't unusual for weird things to be thrown at my window. Aaron had thrown mud balls before, Teddy had thrown gummy worms, Rourk had thrown water balloons, and Jack had thrown some of the tomatoes his dad had grown on their roof. Now someone had thrown an egg, but someone wasn't there. No one was around.

When I turned to ask Jim if he had seen who did it, he was no longer on top of my dresser.

I didn't know what Jim was going to tell me, but I needed to get to the mall and couldn't wait around for him to show up again. I climbed out my window, being careful not to get any egg on myself, and headed across the street to Trevor's. He had told me that he wanted to go to the mall with me to film some of the shops to put into our movie. I was nervous about meeting Janae, so I was kind of happy he wanted to come along. I didn't want to be by myself if she didn't show up or if she brought a friend. It never hurt to have a wingman to help you out. And unlike my other friends, Trevor was a pretty good wingman.

The mall wasn't too far away, but I didn't want to walk. And since my *bike* was broken and my skateboard was in my locked closet, I needed to borrow Trevor's. He never used his skateboard and had only tried it once. His mom had made him wear all kinds of crazy protective gear, and he *still* crashed on a small wall and biffed it bad.

He had fallen down *so* hard that he'd decided never to *skate* again. Now we just used the skateboard to roll each other sodas when we were sitting around his swimming pool.

Trevor lent me his *skateboard*, and he rode his bike. It took him around fifteen minutes to put all of his safety pads on.

By the time we got to the mall, it was almost four and the wind had given me weird hair.

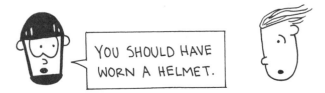

YOU SHOULD HAVE WORN A HELMET.

Trevor also warned me about keeping track of his skateboard. Sure, he never used it, but he still didn't want it to get lost or stolen. He was extra worried because in the last couple of weeks our town, Temon, had been having a lot of little things taken from people's houses and yards. They weren't expensive things. It was more like Kleenex boxes and sunglasses and lawn gnomes. The police were currently looking for what they were calling . . .

THE TEMON TAKER! WE HAVE NO IDEA WHAT THEY LOOK LIKE OR WHO THEY ARE OR WHY THEY TAKE SUCH DUMB THINGS. YOU SHOULD PROBABLY LOCK YOUR DOORS. UNLESS YOU HAVE THINGS YOU WOULD LIKE SOMEONE TO TAKE.

Trevor's family was really concerned about their personal safety, so they had put new locks on their doors and gotten an alarm system. They even put up a sign on their lawn.

I promised Trevor I would keep a good hold on his skateboard and make sure that the Temon Taker didn't get his hands on it.

Since my hair was a mess, we stopped at one of the mall's bathrooms before going to Mustard Burger. I used the mirror in the bathroom and combed through my hair to fix it. Then I nervously made my way with Trevor to Mustard Burger.

IF SHE'S ALONE, TAKE OFF. IF HER FRIENDS ARE THERE, DON'T LEAVE.

WHAT IF SHE'S NOT THERE AND INSTEAD IT'S A DIFFERENT GIRL WHO LIKES ME?

THEN I'LL TAKE OFF AS QUICKLY AS I CAN.

When I got to Mustard Burger, Janae was standing out in front. Okay, so people already make fun of me for the way I described Katfish. And my friends still give me a hard time about once saying Janae was cute, but the thing is, I don't know how to talk about girls. Now, as Janae was standing in front of Mustard Burger, she looked better than ever.

I told Trevor nicely to get lost, and he ran off to film some random stuff. I did my best to walk coolly up to Janae and say,

My mouth needed to be arrested and locked up.

I had said "howdy" as if it was the olden days and we were living in a western town. I quickly added some words after "howdy" in an attempt to make it sound a little less dorky.

Like a fool, I kept talking in an attempt to correct my mistake.

I was about as smooth as a rhino covered in shards of glass.

Janae looked a little concerned at first, but then she smiled and laughed. One of the best things about Janae is that sometimes she mistakes my dorkiness for my sense of humor. So if I say something stupid, she thinks it's just me being clever. I hope she never finds out the truth. I sure as heck am not planning to tell her. I figure I'll wait until I'm on my deathbed to admit things like that.

Janae reached out and took my hand. I think it was because she liked me, or maybe my mom had told her that my balance was poor and I needed people to help prop me up. It kind of seemed like the sort of thing my mom would do.

While holding hands, we bought mustard burgers and fries and sat over by the quarter rides. At first Janae did most of the talking, but every once in a while, I would try to say something that didn't sound too dumb.

Janae and I talked about a lot of things. She was actually pretty easy to have a conversation with. She told me about her life, and I told her about mine. I also told her that my family was going on a trip next week to New Mexico. She was smart enough to know that New Mexico was a state. After I told her about the trip, she said,

OUR NEIGHBORHOOD WILL BE BORING WITHOUT YOU.

I got a compliment from Janae! At least I'm pretty sure it was a compliment. Boring is bad, which means that things will be bad without me. I could feel my neck and face getting hot as I blushed. I must have looked as red as a cherry.

Time flew by, and before I knew it, it was five o'clock and Janae's friend Maggie came looking for her to leave. I didn't know what I should do. I think Janae and I were kind of turning into boyfriend-girlfriend, but nothing was official. Was I supposed to give her a good-bye hug or a kiss? I was so confused that I sort of curtsied.

Of course Maggie laughed at me. And of course I tried to say something to make things better. I don't know what was wrong with me, but my words came out rhyming.

GOOD-BYE TO YOU
GOOD-BYE FROM ME
ILL SHUT UP NOW
BEFORE YOU FLEE.

Janae didn't laugh or smile quite as much as she did earlier. But she did flee. She ran off with Maggie, and I went to look for Trevor. It took me almost twenty minutes to find him. When I did, he was in the Pointy Image store trying out massage chairs.

IT'S BEEN A VERY STRESSFUL WEEK.

NO SITTING!

Trevor and I filmed a few more things for Mr. Mustache and then talked about getting home before our parents got mad at us.

I was going to wait around for Trevor to put on his safety pads, but he started singing his safety song. I took off before he began the second verse.

CHAPTER 6

HAPPY INSTEAD OF SAD

After another boring family dinner . . .

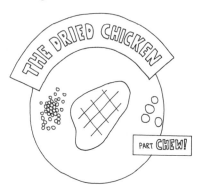

. . . we all went into the family room to watch TV. Right as my favorite show was starting, the doorbell rang.

My mom asked me to get it, so I reluctantly got up and did as I was told. Usually when the doorbell rang, it was one of my friends, so I was typically the one my parents sent to go open the door. It wasn't one of my friends this time. I wasn't actually sure what it was.

I screamed, but I probably shouldn't have, seeing how it was just my aunt Sally. She was wearing a medical mask and a *bathrobe* and breathing like Darth Vader with a cold. She didn't want to come in because she was

SUPER CONTAGIOUS. THAT MEANS I'LL GET YOU SICK IF YOU GET TOO CLOSE.

I didn't want to get any closer. I yelled for my dad and mom, and they came running to *see* what all the ruckus was about. The good news was . . . I mean the *bad* news was that my cousin Kyle had just come down with something called swamp fever, and now my uncle Paul had it and my aunt Sally probably did too. That was super sad, but even happier . . . I mean even sadder, they weren't going to be able to go on the trip with us next week.

I think my mom was okay with that. She kept smiling really big while she was telling my aunt Sally how sorry she was that they were sick.

My mom didn't always get along with my aunt Sally. They had a disagreement a year ago about how people should raise their kids. I guess my mom thought that Kyle was a little out of control and that my aunt needed to discipline him a little more.

They got along a little better these days, but I could tell my mom was happy that she wouldn't *be* trapped in an RV for a week with my aunt, Uncle Paul, and their wild kid, Kyle.

WE ARE SO SAD.

My dad was the most upset, although you couldn't really tell because he always looked excited. He was worried about my aunt, but he was most concerned about who would use the three extra train tickets and the extra hotel room. Libby had an idea.

CAN I BRING MELANY?

Melany was Maggie's big sister. She was also Libby's best friend. I liked her a little more than I liked Libby. She was loud and always talking about her boyfriend, Roy.

I told my parents that it wasn't fair for Libby to bring Melany, because I couldn't bring Trevor. Surprisingly, my mom said Trevor could go if his parents gave him permission. My dad jokingly asked Tuffin if he wanted to bring a friend, and he said,

Tuffin liked Jack. I think it's because once when my mom got a bunch of whipped cream from the warehouse club store, Jack borrowed a couple of bottles and accidentally covered Tuffin with them while he was helping me babysit.

I don't know if my parents were woozy from the dry chicken we had for dinner or if they had been replaced by aliens, but for some reason, they both agreed that I could bring Trevor and Jack, and Libby could bring Melany on our trip.

IF THEIR PARENTS SAY IT'S OKAY.

Libby and I didn't waste a moment going to ask. We both knew that my mom could change her mind in an instant. I ran out the front door across the street to Trevor's house, and Libby called Melany. At Trevor's house, I rang the doorbell ten times.

DING⌐ DING⌐ DING⌐ DING⌐ DING⌐
  DING⌐ DING⌐ DING⌐ DING⌐ DING⌐
                                    DING!

Trevor answered the door wearing a paint smock. He was busy painting some scenery for *Mustache and the Mighty Cool Adventure.*

GOOD NEWS, MY COUSIN GOT SICK AND NOW MY PARENTS SAID I CAN BRING YOU ON THE TRIP TO NEW MEXICO NEXT WEEK IF YOUR PARENTS SAY OKAY.

EEEEEEEEEEKKK!

After he got done squealing, I told Trevor all the details. We would be leaving in a couple of days, we would be gone a week, and we would be riding in an RV. He was a little worried that his parents wouldn't let him miss a week of school. That was a problem, so I told him to tell his parents that it was going to be super-educational and that we would be stopping at a bunch of landmarks and would get to ride a train. Plus, my mom would probably force us to sing songs about math. I also told Trevor that I was going to invite Jack as well.

I WON'T TELL THEM THAT PART.

Trevor ran off to ask his parents while I stood outside his front door. It seemed like forever, but finally he burst back out.

I couldn't believe it. My life was really going well. Janae and I were kind of an item. Even though I didn't know what kind of item exactly, but we were one.

And now I got to miss a week of school and go on a trip in an RV with my friends instead of my wonderful . . . I mean awful cousin, Kyle. Ever since Kat had come and gone, things were going swimmingly.

We ran over to Jack's house and rang the doorbell at least twenty times. His older brother answered the door and gave us an evil glare.

Jack's big brother was nice on some days and mean on others. He was in high school and used to be a star football player. But last year he had an accident on the field, and now he had a bum knee. I'm not really sure what that even means.

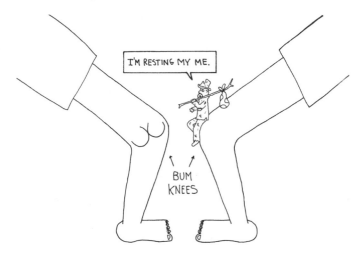

A few weeks ago, Jack's big brother had started his own business making T-shirts. Not many people bought them because they were dumb.

When he wasn't making T-shirts, he was throwing rocks at things, and *because of that*, he was always getting in trouble for throwing rocks at things. Last week he threw a rock at a window of the Awful House, and Aaron's mom had seen him do it. So he was grounded for a few days. Now he was trying to act nice. He almost smiled and then went off to get Jack. When Jack came to the door, he was holding an old Barbie and a bottle of barbecue sauce.

ARE YOU OKAY?

I'M WORKING ON MY SCIENCE PROJECT.

I told Jack about the trip and how Tuffin had asked that he come along. I told him we'd get to miss a week of school and that we would *be* driving in an RV.

I told Jack that my whole family was going and that Libby was bringing a friend. I asked him if he wanted to come.

Jack's family life was a little different than mine. He could stay out later, watch movies that were scarier, and use words around his parents that my mom wouldn't approve of.

Apparently he could also go with his friends on weeklong trips to another state without asking permission.

This was going to be a great trip.

CHAPTER 7

RECREATIONAL VEHICLE

My other friends were pretty upset that they
hadn't been invited to come to New Mexico. I tried
to tell them I was sorry and that I could only bring
one person and Tuffin had picked Jack, but they
weren't accepting it.

I couldn't take them, and there was nothing I could do about it. My dad had won a trip for eight people, and they would make nine, ten, and eleven.

Trevor promised to film a ton of footage so that when we got back we could edit it into one epic mustache movie for everyone to watch.

The night *before* we were going to leave on our trip, my dad came home with the RV he had rented.

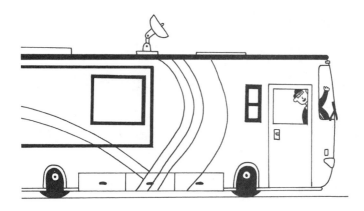

It was huge and way better than our house. There were two TVs, a kitchen, bedrooms, and a ladder you could climb to go through a hatch and get up on the roof.

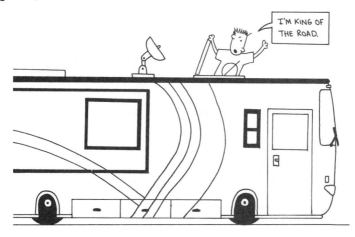

I'M KING OF THE ROAD.

Teddy, Aaron, and Rourk were even more upset now. They had never been in an RV, and it seemed like me and Trevor and Jack were going to be traveling in some cool, fun, futuristic vehicle.

Even though we all knew Aaron had never ridden in a recreational vehicle, he started saying some of his normal lies to make it sound like he had, and that he wasn't all that impressed we were going to be going in one.

None of us were impressed. We really didn't even listen to him, but all of my friends did help me explore the RV until Teddy broke one of the knobs off of a cabinet and my dad asked him politely to get out and . . .

GO HOME.

My dad then instructed me, Trevor, and Jack to go pack and bring our stuff so that he could get it into the RV and make sure everything was ready for tomorrow. Trevor and Jack ran to their homes, and I took off to my room. It didn't take me too long to pack, but I got the feeling that Beardy was watching me as I moved around my room.

He didn't reply. I was starting to think he might never open up again. Maybe Katfish was the last creature that would ever come out. She could have been wrong when she said it was going to get weirder. Maybe she meant it would get weirder like Janae would stop hating me and I would get to go on a trip with some of my friends.

For some reason, Beardy didn't look as sure about that explanation as I did. It kind of seemed like he was rolling his eyes at me.

When I made it back to the RV, Trevor and Jack were ready with their stuff. Trevor had his suitcase, I had my duffel bag, and Jack had something else.

TREVOR'S SUITCASE   MY DUFFEL BAG   JACK'S TRASH BAG

Trevor had packed tons of extra stuff like hand-powered flashlights, a safety whistle in case he got separated from my family, and twelve pairs of underwear, even though we were only going to be gone seven days.

ACCIDENTS HAPPEN.

My dad put our things in the storage bins at the bottom of the RV. He then told my friends to go home and . . .

GET A GOOD SLEEP.
IT MAKES YOU WELL.
VITAMIN ZZZZZZ
IS BETTER THAN PILLS.

Trevor thanked my dad for the great advice and Jack said,

THERE'S A TRIBE IN THE
AMAZON THAT NEVER SLEEPS.

My dad was pretty worried about the tribe. He started to ask Jack all sorts of questions, so Jack decided to leave. That left just me, my dad, and

Tuffin to talk about the people in the Amazon who never slept.

In my dad's mind, the world would be a perfect place as long as everyone had enough slides and swings. I helped my dad pack a few more things into the RV and then went to my room to get ready for bed. We were going to leave at six in the morning. I changed into one of my dad's old concert shirts and got in bed. As I was lying there, it looked like Beardy was glowing. What? Could this be happening?!

I was going out of town for a week. Now would
not be a good time for Beardy to unlock himself.
I couldn't care for another creature at the moment.
I needed things to be calm. No distractions.
Tomorrow was going to be the beginning of a fun
time—no worries for over a week. I looked at my
window and realized that it was the reflection of the
setting sun that was making Beardy glow. Phew! I
fell asleep quickly, knowing that everything was
perfect.

CHAPTER 8

ON THE ROAD

Tuffin was even more excited for the trip than I was. He woke me up early the next morning by breathing in my face and staring at me as I slept.

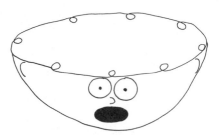

It was five o'clock, so I rolled out of bed and stretched as big as I could to wake myself up.

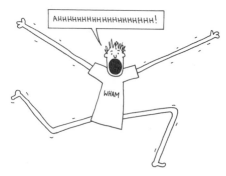

The rest of my family was already up. Libby was in the bathroom getting ready, my mom was making food for the trip in the kitchen, and my dad was wearing what looked like a train conductor's hat with a scarf around his neck.

As soon as Libby was done with the bathroom, I got ready. Then I helped Tuffin pack a few toys to bring. He wanted to take a bunch of things that weren't very practical.

I talked him into taking just a few little cars and a stuffed animal. At quarter to six, Trevor and Jack were at my front door knocking. Trevor had a hat and bandanna on too.

Jack had a shirt with Beardy on the front of it to match the Beardy burned into his palm.

It was pretty early, but our driveway was packed. Trevor's parents had come to see their son off. They were acting like he was going to war. Jack's dad was there, but I think it was just to make sure Jack was actually leaving. Aaron and Teddy were there to see if by some chance things had changed and they could come. Melany, Libby's friend, was there with her suitcase and ready to go. Melany's sister, Maggie, had come to see her off, and standing next to Maggie was Janae. I was really glad I had showered and gotten ready. It was quite a crowd.

I walked over to Janae as my mom gave our house keys to Trevor's mom so she could feed Puck and Fred while we were gone. I looked at Janae and smiled.

Janae told me to have fun and that she would miss me. Janae was going to miss me? This was crazy. I had a hard time believing I wasn't dreaming or that the universe wasn't messed up, pushing the planets out of whack.

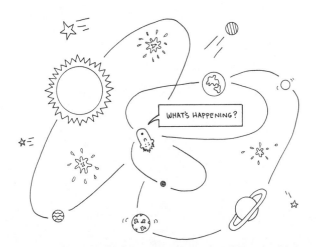

To make things even stranger, Janae gave me one of her necklaces to wear so that I would remember her. Was she crazy? There was no way I would forget her. Still, I took the necklace and promised I would wear it. I was glad that it looked more like a boy necklace than a girl one.

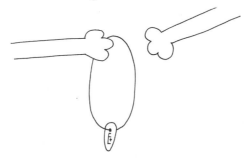

Trevor's mom was big-time into scrapbooking, so she insisted that everyone who was going on the trip gather together for a group picture.

After we took the picture, my dad climbed into the RV and honked the horn. We all got in and waved at everyone standing in the driveway. As my dad was backing out and I was waving at Janae, I heard something sneeze in one of the small cabinets by the table. I knew that there shouldn't be sneezing coming from there, so I opened it up to see . . .

Rourk was acting confused and weirder than usual. My dad stopped the vehicle so that our stowaway could get off. Rourk stepped down the stairs looking sad. My dad closed the door and we drove off, but not before my mom had us check to make sure that some other friend wasn't hiding in some other cabinet.

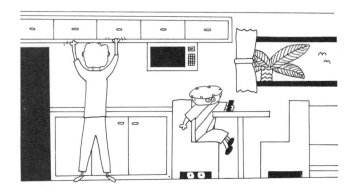

By the time we finally got moving, it was five minutes after six. My dad was a little upset that we were getting off to a late start, but he tried to sing himself out of it.

NOBODY'S PERFECT. WE LIVE AND WE LEARN IT.

The RV was really big, but after we had been driving an hour, it started to feel a little small. Libby and Melany were hogging the big bed in the back to watch a movie about an ice skater who lost his foot. My mom was sleeping in the passenger seat, and Tuffin was strapped in at the kitchen table playing with Play-Doh. Trevor was filming scenery that we drove past, and Jack had already used the bathroom three times.

To make things worse, my mom was supposed to pack our video game system and a bunch of games and movies for us. But when we pulled out the box, there were just books. And the only ones were the Lord of the Rings trilogy and a bunch of Dr. Seuss books for Tuffin. My mom swore she had packed the other stuff, but we couldn't find it anywhere. She was also confused because the books that were in the box had all come from the public library.

I figured my mom had just forgotten, since sometimes parents are forgetful. But something about the books in the box made me nervous. I picked up *Marvin K. Mooney Will You Please Go Now!* and flipped through it. I loved Dr. Seuss books when I was little, but I hadn't read one in years. And I loved the Lord of the Rings and the Hobbit movies, but the books were really long, and there was no way I was going to spend the trip reading. As far as I was concerned, I was on vacation from *books* and from my closet.

So the RV seemed a little cramped, and we didn't have any games or movies to watch, but we did have my dad and his lame driving games.

Another thing about RVs that's not that great is how slow you have to drive. My dad was already a slow driver, but he had to go even slower in the RV. We were driving so slow that when the road became a two-lane highway, we had at least a hundred cars behind us honking and wishing we would go faster.

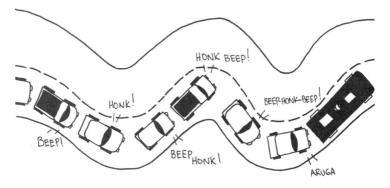

We made our first stop for gas in a town called Myron, Arizona. It wasn't much of a town, but the truck stop was huge. My parents encouraged everyone to use the bathrooms so we didn't overuse the one in the RV. I think they were mainly talking to Jack, because no one else had used it yet. Everyone got out and went into the truck stop while my dad filled the RV with more gas and whistled a song about filling up.

I had never been to a truck stop before, and the bathrooms were weird. There were showers right in the bathrooms. I guess truckers that drove cross-country needed a place to clean up too. Because of that, there were some truckers in towels standing in the bathroom waiting to shower.

Luckily we didn't have to hold it or use the RV's. Not far from the regular bathroom there was a family bathroom.

I used it first. It had paintings of friendly animals and a diaper changing table that folded out and a big thing of hand sanitizer. There were also all kinds of simple signs explaining things.

Trevor used the bathroom after me, and Jack used it after him. When Jack came out, he said,

We made our way to the RV quickly, and right before we climbed inside, Jack asked,

It took us three more hours of driving before we arrived at the RV campground. During those three hours, not much happened. My dad honked the horn like mad when we crossed over the New Mexico

border, and I read a lot of Dr. Seuss books to
Tuffin as Jack and Trevor played cards with Libby
and Melany. The RV campground was kind of cool.
It was right next to some mountains and a big river.
After we parked, my parents gave us two orders.

Libby and Melany went to see if there were any
cute boys traveling with other families at the RV
park. My mom started to prepare dinner with
Tuffin's help, and my dad set up some folding chairs
and built a fire near the back of the RV. Me and
my friends headed into the woods to film stuff.

I put my mustache on, and we filmed Jack and me sword-fighting with sticks for *Mustache and the Mighty Cool Adventure.*

When it started getting dark, we returned to the RV to find everyone sitting around the fire eating Lunchables and Hot Pockets.

We ate and sang some songs, and then me and Jack tossed a football around while Trevor showed my dad some of the rocks he found. Libby and Melany went back into the RV to talk about Roy, and Tuffin fell asleep in my mom's arms. After Jack accidentally beaned me in the head with the football for the seventh time, we decided to stop doing that and watch some of the stuff we had filmed earlier. We just watched it on the camera. It was a small screen, so we walked away from the firelight to see better.

While I was watching one of the scenes, I thought I saw something odd.

Trevor replayed the video, and I saw it again. In the background, some red and white stripes were moving behind a bush.

Trevor and Jack squinted and examined the video carefully. We replayed it a dozen times, but it still wasn't clear what it was.

My heart *began* to beat faster. I had recently had some experience with unidentified little things coming from my closet. It seemed impossible that something that had to do with my closet could *be so* far from my house, but *impossible* was a word I was believing in less and less these days.

My mom took Tuffin back to the RV to tuck him in for the night. He was mumbling a bunch of things that didn't make sense.

My dad started yawning and talking about . . .

There was room for me and my friends to bunk inside the RV, but we had brought sleeping bags so that we could stay outside. My dad grabbed the sleeping bags and gave them to us. He told us how to tend the fire and said to have a good night. We placed our sleeping bags around the fire and crawled into them.

I was happy to be on the trip. I was happy to be sleeping outside with my friends. I was also more than a little curious about what I had seen on Trevor's camera. We talked and belched and acted like kids should in the wild. It was a nice moment. As I drifted off, I thought I heard something in the wind.

CHAPTER 9

BUMPS IN THE NIGHT

I didn't sleep well. It was cold and Jack snores—a lot. I also kept hearing things. I wanted to wake my friends up and go into the RV, but I knew they would make fun of me for years. So I slept poorly, and when I woke up, the first thing I said was,

I was uneasy. There was something going on, and I couldn't quite put my finger on it. My rhyming was not normal. The ULT I saw on the film was unusual. I knew that something was happening, but how could Beardy and my closet be messing with me so far from home? It wasn't like they could just phone it in.

After breakfast we drove for two hours and stopped at the world's biggest toothpick to take a picture.

We then drove another three hours and had a lunch of fried chicken near the world's largest collection of dice.

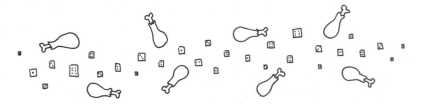

Then we drove about three more hours and reached our destination for the night in the town of Simmering, New Mexico. We stopped at another RV park near a drive-in movie theater that was no longer in operation.

We had dinner around another campfire, and my dad filled us in on what would be happening tomorrow.

WE WILL BE TAKING THE TRAIN TOMORROW MORNING. IT'S A FIVE-HOUR RIDE UP TO THE TOP OF THE MOUNTAINS, WHERE WE WILL BE STAYING IN ONE OF AMERICA'S OLDEST HOTELS.

GROSS.

My dad said that it was also one of the grandest. We would be in the town of Tolk for two nights. There would be horseback riding and tennis and hiking.

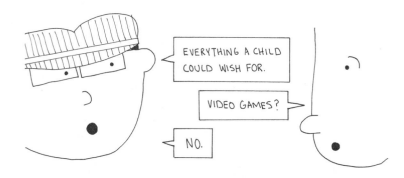

EVERYTHING A CHILD COULD WISH FOR.

VIDEO GAMES?

NO.

He then added that on the second night he would
be honored with an award for the outstanding small
business by the governor of New Mexico. This was
a family vacation, yes—but this was really about my
dad getting his award, and if we wanted to have any
fun we couldn't ruin this for him. So I said,

When everyone was done eating, my dad
suggested that we all hike over to the abandoned
drive-in theater and see if there were any ghosts. I
loved abandoned buildings. My grandpa once gave
me a book that was filled with pictures of buildings
that had been abandoned. They were all interesting
and creepy-looking. Now I would get to explore an

old drive-in. I was okay with that. So after dinner we cleaned up and walked as a group out of the RV park, across a road, and up to the drive-in. It was kind of a scary night, and Libby and Melany were acting more frightened than Tuffin. At the drive-in there was a rope holding an old gate closed. My dad pulled the rope, and the gate opened. We walked in to where cars used to park to watch movies. I could see the weathered old screen in the distance. Trevor started to panic.

I suggested we all run back to the RV and get the camera together, but my dad seemed to think it would be fine for me and Trevor to go alone. Tuffin wouldn't let Jack come, so it was just us two. We crossed the road and worked our way through the RV park. When we got to our RV, I heard something moving around inside. Trevor was about to blow the emergency safety whistle he was wearing when I said,

I pointed toward the RV. There was a light on inside, and we could see the silhouette of something. Trevor adjusted his glasses.

Trevor really wanted to blow his safety whistle, but I wouldn't let him. I had a pretty good idea of what we were looking at. I didn't think it was an accident that we ended up with nothing but Lord of the Rings books and Dr. Seuss stuff. I also thought there was a reason why I was rhyming so much lately. I told Trevor that I thought it was possible that Beardy had set something free from my closet and it had traveled with us here. I also told him that if I had to guess, I thought it might be part Dr. Seuss, part Lord of the Rings.

Trevor no longer wanted to blow his whistle. He wanted to open the RV door and get a look. Trevor loved the Lord of the Rings books. He had read them a couple of times. He also loved Dr. Seuss.

We could hear something knocking things over in the RV. We could also hear it saying,

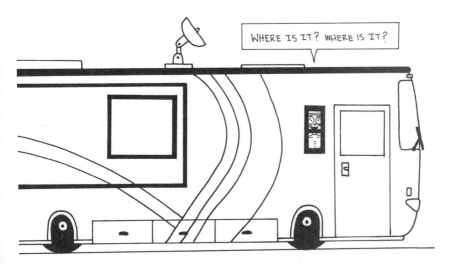

I wished my dad was there, but I knew that I couldn't go get him, because if the creature was from my closet, it would probably be best that my parents didn't know. They had no clue what my closet could do, and they'd be blue if they ever knew.

I opened the RV door and looked inside. There was a dish on the floor, and one of the cabinets was hanging open.

This is a good example of how different my life had become. In the past I never would have gone into an RV with something strange knocking about in it. Now it was almost normal to be surrounded by strange.

I stepped into the RV and looked around. One light was on, but there were shadows everywhere. Trevor stepped in behind me. He had his hands and arms up over his face for protection.

TELL THEM WE MEAN NO HARM.

YOU TELL THEM.

Before either one of us could tell anyone anything, something popped out of a cabinet and flew toward us.

HELLO!

We both screamed and fell backward. The creature hopped onto the small counter near the stove. From what I could see, it looked like it was part Cat in the Hat and part Gollum. He was wearing a hat, a loincloth, and a red bow tie. Trevor knelt down as if in awe.

YOUR HONOR.

YOU'RE ODD.

Trevor stood up, and the creature jumped from the counter onto his shoulder. Trevor looked pretty happy about that. I had a few questions I needed to ask:

This was not good. When Katfish had come from my closet, I had been confused because she seemed to just be a character from one book, *The Hunger Games*. It wasn't until she jumped in my pool that I discovered she was part mermaid, and her other half was from *The Little Mermaid*. This new character seemed to be parts of three characters. In the Lord of the Rings, Gollum was also Sméagol. Gollum was the mean crazy half, and Sméagol was the nice crazy half. And now those two personalities had added a slice of rhyming Cat in the Hat.

As confusing as the characters in the past had been, none of them had used words like *doo-wuzzle-ee*. Trevor told me that *doo-wuzzle-ee* means "good" in Elvish from Lord of the Rings. I told him he was nuts. I asked our new creature if he was here to help, and he said "sort of," which made me sort of uneasy. I asked him where he had been hiding in the RV, and he said "under," which made me understand that he was not going to give me straightforward answers. I questioned him about what I needed to do before he could return to the closet, and he screamed,

MY PURR-ECIOUS!

The creature jumped down from the refrigerator and dashed under the kitchen table. He grabbed something off of the floor and looked up, smiling.

There, in his palm, was a ring. I thought Trevor was going to have a geek attack. Ever since I had

known Trevor, he had loved Lord of the Rings, and now here was some sort of Kitty Gollum holding a ring in his palm. The creature put the ring in a pocket that was sewn into the fabric around his waist. I could see that there were other rings in the pocket as well. He patted the pocket, jumped on top of the refrigerator, and said,

I wasn't sure I cared for the rhyming, but the creature was interesting. It would be a difficult task to make sure nobody saw him until we got back to

my house and I could hide him in a drawer or backpack. But so far he seemed willing to stay out of the way. If he could keep that up, it would make things much easier. I just didn't want him ruining the trip for my dad.

IF YOU COULD KEEP HIDDEN, THAT WOULD BE GREAT. THIS TRIP MEANS A LOT TO MY FATHER.

IS HE PRECIOUS?

I GUESS SO. THAT'S JUST NOT SOMETHING MIDDLE SCHOOL KIDS SAY ABOUT THEIR DADS.

I DO.

The little creature promised he would do all he could to make our quest successful. Of course he said it in a rhyme and with some made-up words like *koodumpfoomagoo*. I thanked him and opened the door to the RV. The creature climbed up the side of the RV and disappeared over the top.

When me and Trevor got back to the abandoned drive-in, my dad had propped up a flashlight and they were casting shadows against the old screen. Libby and Melany were currently acting out some scene from a movie.

I didn't love it. Plus, I was thinking about Seussol. Trevor was preoccupied as well. We had already experienced some really cool things as a result of my closet visitors, but this new creature was extra exciting. I grew up on Dr. Seuss books, and the Lord of the Rings movies were on my favorite list. Even though Gollum sort of freaked me out, the part of him that was here was way less frightening. His small size was cool, and he was like a stuffed animal that someone had sewn together wrong.

After messing around at the theater for a while, we all walked back to the RV and roasted marshmallows. It was nice until Jack accidentally threw one of his shoes into the fire.

UM...OOPS?

The smell of rubber burning caused everyone besides me and my friends to call it a night. The three of us laid out our sleeping bags around the fire and fell asleep to the smell of Jack's burning shoe and the knowledge that somewhere out there Seussol was keeping his eye on things.

I'M WATCHING YOU, MR. SNICKER-WAA-ZOO.

MR. SNICKER-WAA-ZOO IS MY FATHER. PLEASE, CALL ME TOBY.

CHAPTER 10

ALL ABOARD

Because Jack hadn't snored as loud, and because it wasn't as cold, I slept a lot better than the night before.

My dad cooked everyone a breakfast of burnt eggs and Spam.

He then kept talking about how great food tastes in the outdoors.

I'm pretty sure most kings don't have to choke down eggs like that.

When breakfast was over, we cleaned up our site and drove away from the RV park.

I don't know why Jack threw his left shoe into the fire, but then again I never really understand half the things Jack does.

Now Jack had only one shoe, and we were going to have to find him some new ones at the next stop. There was no way he could go the rest of the trip with only one shoe.

You CAN BORROW ONE OF MINE. I BROUGHT A SPARE PAIR.

NO OFFENSE, BUT YOUR SHOES ARE TOO BORING FOR ME.

It was a short drive to our next destination, the town of Broken Wagon, New Mexico. From there we were going to take a train up into the mountains where our hotel would be. My dad parked the RV by the train station, and we got our stuff out to take with us. I was more than a little shocked when I saw what Tuffin was wearing as a backpack.

While getting stuff out of the compartments at
the bottom of the RV, my mom found Seussol!
And instead of assuming it was a strange creature
from her son's closet, she thought it was a child's
backpack that belonged to Tuffin. Trevor and I had
a difficult time not freaking out about it. Seussol
just winked at us.

WHAT ARE WE GOING TO DO?

I DON'T KNOW.

ARE YOU STILL WORRIED ABOUT MY BURNT SHOE?

This trip was beginning to worry me. Yes, I had
wanted to ride on a train, but that was before I
knew I would be having to keep an eye on Tuffin's
backpack. It wasn't easy keeping track of
something with a will of its own. My closet was
messing with me again.

A pretty cool train pulled into the station. It was an old-fashioned train with ten cars, and supposedly super-famous, but I hadn't heard of it before. Of course Trevor had.

The train station was not very busy. I thought there would be a crowd of small businessmen gathered around waiting to ride into the mountains and to the hotel. But it was really just us. My dad gave our eight tickets to a woman sitting behind a glass window, and she let us through a little spinning bar. We all got on, and a man wearing a hat like my dad's and Trevor's came into the car and told us a few things we needed to know. He didn't seem very happy.

WELCOME TO OL'STEAMY, THE WORLD'S STEAMIEST STEAM ENGINE. I'M WALLY, AND FOR THE NEXT FOUR HOURS I WILL BE YOUR CONDUCTOR.

Trevor blew his whistle in excitement, and Wally told him that blowing a whistle when there wasn't an emergency was a violation of over a dozen train rules.

SORRY.

WHISTLES ARE A RESPONSIBILITY AND A PRIVILEGE.

A GREAT PRIVILEGE.

After Conductor Wally gave us about a hundred other rules to follow, he reluctantly told us that we were allowed to explore the train and visit the dining car, but that he . . .

WOULD PREFER YOU ALL SIT STILL THE WHOLE TIME.

That was not going to happen. I had never been on a train before, so there was no way I was going to sit still the whole time. I also knew that even if my mom said we had to, my dad would let us run around, because he was almost as excited.

Wally told us he would *be* sitting in a chair near the front of the train if we needed him. He then exited the car. *The* second Wally was gone, me and my friends began to search the train. I couldn't leave Seussol, so I volunteered to take Tuffin with us because the creature was still strapped to his back. My mom looked really happy.

We ran off with Tuffin to explore the caboose. There were open windows and lots of seats in the other cars.

Trevor filmed everything, and Jack kept stopping to point out things that he had never done before on a train.

We all sat down in the caboose, and I asked Tuffin if I could borrow his backpack for a moment. He said no. So I asked him if I could talk to his backpack. He had no problem with that. He turned around so Seussol faced us. The little guy saw Jack's Beardy shirt and began to wig out. Jack saw Seussol and did some wigging out of his own.

Trevor put down his camera and explained to Jack about how we had discovered Seussol last night. And I told Jack that we needed to keep him hidden until we got home and figured out why Seussol was here.

HE'S NOT VERY HIDDEN.

I KNOW.

THIS IS THE FIRST TIME I'VE TALKED TO A BACKPACK ON A TRAIN.

I talked with Seussol for a few more minutes while Jack kept Tuffin distracted so he wouldn't turn around and cut off our conversation. I wasn't so worried about Tuffin ruining the conversation as I was Seussol. Talking to someone with three personalities was exhausting, and one of the personalities rhymed, so that made it even more confusing.

Seussol was not at all helpful. He was pathetic and clever at the same time. I had read a bunch of Dr. Seuss books to Tuffin yesterday. I had even read some aloud last night to Trevor by the fire.

But I hadn't read the Lord of the Rings. The books were so thick it would take me half a year to finish the series. There was no way Seussol could hang around half a year. I was already missing my calm life from a couple of days ago.

WILL YOU TELL ME WHY YOU'RE HERE?

NO.

WHAT IF I CAN'T FIGURE IT OUT?

THEN THE AGE OF MAN WILL BE OVER.

REALLY?

NO.

Seussol let go of Tuffin's neck, and before any of us knew what he was doing, he pulled seven rings from his pocket.

Then Seussol slipped one of the rings on his
finger. In an instant he was gone. It was almost like
he disappeared into thin air. He was invisible. Tuffin
didn't like the disappearance of his new backpack.
He started to scream and shout while we all called
out. It sounded like an episode of *Dora the
Explorer.*

Tuffin kept crying until I promised I would find his backpack and buy him ice cream from the dining car. He accepted my offer, and we worked our way through the train, stopping only once for Jack.

CHAPTER 11

TRAINING

I don't know what moves slower up mountains, RVs
or trains. As we wound up the mountain, the train
was going so slow I could practically step off it and
then step back on.

It was fun to be on a train, but after an hour it wasn't that great. There was nobody else on it, which made *sense* because any smart person would have just driven. One good thing did happen. While I was looking for Seussol, I felt something hop onto my right shoulder and hold on to my neck. That same something then whispered,

HELLO, MASTER ROBBIT.
I'M RIGHT HERE.

I have always wanted a monkey to sit on my shoulder, so I was pretty pleased to have an invisible Seussol hanging out on mine. Him being there made the boring train ride seem a lot better. I had secretly hoped we would be zipping up the mountain and people on horses would be shooting guns and trying to rob us. Instead it seemed like we were trapped on a really long nature ride.

There were only two things that made it exciting: One was the fact that Seussol was riding on me while no one could see him. The other was the dining car. It was fun eating food on a train, even though some of the food was disgusting.

Jack dared me to eat one of the gross pickled eggs floating around in a jar, but I refused. Then he followed me around, asking,

WOULD YOU EAT THIS ON A TRAIN
THAT'S KIND OF LAME,
WITH A DUMB-SOUNDING NAME?

I WILL NOT EAT IT ON A TRAIN
THAT'S KIND OF LAME,
WITH A DUMB-SOUNDING NAME.
I WILL NOT EAT IT ANYWHERE,
NOT ON A WHIM, OR ON A DARE.
I NEVER WANT TO SEE THAT SNACK,
SO KNOCK IT OFF THIS INSTANT, JACK!

I could hear Seussol laughing on my shoulder. I guess he was happy about how me and Jack were talking.

HEY, THAT'S MY FIRST TIME
RHYMING ON A TRAIN.

One of the train cars had some bunk beds in it. Probably because the train ride was so slow and long that people needed to take naps. We weren't tired, but we all went to the bunk car and stretched out on a bed. I took a top bunk, and the moment I was on mine, Seussol appeared in the flesh.

Seussol took off. I was really happy about him wanting to talk. I desperately needed to find out why he was here and what I needed to do to help. I also wanted to make it clear to him that I wouldn't be reading the Lord of the Rings trilogy because the books seemed too thick and heavy.

After a couple of minutes, I began complaining that my stomach hurt. I then excused myself to go and use the bathroom.

I didn't think bathrooms could be *fun*, but I made my way down the bunk car, through the dining cart, and over to the bathroom. I opened the door and kept it open for a couple of seconds so that if Seussol wasn't already in there, he could slip inside. Libby walked by with Melany, and they saw me standing there in the bathroom doorway.

YOU HANG OUT IN AWFUL PLACES.

I didn't really care if Libby thought I was nuts, but Melany's little sister, Maggie, was friends with Janae, and I didn't want Melany going back and telling her sister about me spending time in the bathroom. So I said something dumb.

Libby and Melany laughed at me the way a heartless person might laugh at an orphan on the streets who just tripped while selling matches.

I slipped into the bathroom and closed the door. Seussol took off his ring and materialized on the sink. He smiled at me and I smiled back. It was cool to see him. He seemed even more mixed up

than the other creatures I had gotten to hang out
with in the last few months.

Seussol nodded. Apparently when he had the ring
on, my mom was the only one who seemed to sense
he was around. She kept staring at him even though
she couldn't see him.

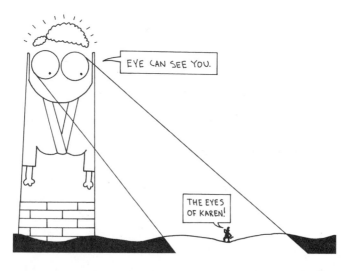

I asked Seussol what the quest was he had talked about, and he showed me one of the rings. He said that he must get it to the fire in the mountains where it came from. He then said something curious.

IT'S THE SAME PLACE WHERE BEARDY WAS FORGED.

I had never really thought about where Beardy had come from. He was a doorknob, and in my mind he had just always existed. I knew he was special, because he was the gatekeeper to all the things that my closet created.

BUT WHY DO YOU HAVE TO BRING THE RING?

NICE RHYME.

THANKS.

IT MUST BE RETURNED TO THE FIRE TO CREATE SOMETHING NEW.

My heart started racing. Never had a creature come from my closet with such a cool quest. Returning a ring to a great fire was something I was definitely okay with. I would help Seussol and in doing so, help Beardy.

I talked to Seussol in the bathroom for almost half an hour. He let me pick him up and told me all kinds of important things about my closet that I didn't know. He said there were many book mash-ups just waiting to come out. He mentioned Wonk and

Hairy and Pinocula. He also said that Katfish
was doing well. According to him, the reason my
closet made such fantastical creatures was
because of the combination of books and old fake
lab supplies, but Beardy was the key to making it
all work.

THAT'S WHY THIS QUEST
IS SO IMPORTANT.

After I'd been talking to Seussol for a while, my
mom knocked on the bathroom door.

ARE YOU OKAY?
YOU'VE BEEN IN
THERE A LONG
TIME.

ALMOST DONE.

RESTROOM

When I came out of the bathroom with an invisible Seussol, I could see through the windows that the train was pulling into a small town. A few tiny stores popped into view.

My dad was so excited. I was scared that he was going to explode. I knew that this trip meant a lot to him, but I also knew that it meant a lot to me. I know closets don't normally act like mine. And now I was going to figure out something about Beardy.

We just needed to find Bartholomew's Hat and the
fire that burned on top of it.

CHAPTER 12

THE TOWN OF TOLK

I could barely tell when the train stopped because it was going so slow in the first place.

We all got off and thanked the cranky conductor for a really long ride. The town of Tolk was beautiful. A lot of famous people came here to relax or get away from it all. There were huge pine trees and mountains that looked proud to be placed where they were. There was an old-fashioned-looking Main Street with a lot of stores on it.

The hotel we were staying at was almost directly across the street from the train station. So we just carried our stuff over the road and up to the front door.

The hotel looked too fancy to be located in the town of Tolk. It had shiny gold trim around all the window edges, and a huge front entrance where a man in a long coat held the door open for us.

RIGHT THIS WAY.

It was even fancier inside the hotel. There were all kinds of paintings and chandeliers. There were also rugs so soft and thick that I almost got stuck in one.

In the lobby, there was a little sign welcoming all the members of the small business groups. My dad had my mom take his picture by it.

When we checked in, the man at the counter said that my dad was the honored guest, so we got some of the best rooms in the hotel. My dad was so happy, he looked like he was going to pass out from joy. I kept glancing around nervously. I was worried that someone might find out Seussol was on my shoulder. Occasionally I would see my mom stare at me as if something was wrong. So I stepped away from my parents to study the tourist pamphlets the hotel had available for the taking.

I was super happy to find the one I needed. I took it and stared at the picture on the front. I was speechless! Bartholomew's Hat looked just like . . .

It was a small stone mountain shaped like a hat with the face of Beardy carved into the side of it. I put the pamphlet into my pocket and joined my family. I didn't know what was happening, but I felt pretty sure that nobody else in the world was dealing with the surprise of finding out that the face on their closet doorknob was also carved on the side of a stone hill in New Mexico.

Our rooms were really nice. It seemed more like the kind of place a president or movie star would stay, not a playground salesman's family. When I told my dad this, he said,

After everyone cleaned up, we had dinner at the hotel restaurant. It was packed with smart people who had probably driven up in their cars instead of taking the slow train. During dinner my dad told us some of the fun things we could do tomorrow:

WE CAN RIDE HORSES. THERE ARE TWO MUSEUMS. THERE'S A PETTING ZOO. THERE'S ALSO A POND WHERE WE CAN SKIP ROCKS AND FEED THE DUCKS.

PLAY TODAY

My dad rattled off a ton of ideas. Libby and Melany wanted to go to the outlet mall, and my mom and Tuffin wanted to go to the petting zoo. I knew exactly what I needed to do and exactly how to ask for it.

I GUESS I'LL DO WHATEVER YOU GUYS WANT. I JUST REALLY HOPED TO GET SOME EXERCISE AND CLIMB TO THE TOP OF BARTHOLOMEW'S HAT.

BARTHOLOMEW'S HAT?

PLAY TODAY

I handed the pamphlet I had picked up over to my dad. He loved the idea. He was pretty keen on fitness and the outdoors. So the plan was for the girls to go shopping, my mom and Tuffin to go zooing, and the rest of us to hike to Bartholomew's Hat. Then, when the hike was over, we would come back and my dad would get ready for his ceremony. I think Seussol was happy with the itinerary, because he kept whispering in my ear.

PERFECT, MASTER ROBBIT, PERFECT.

After dinner we walked to a store for Jack to buy some new shoes. He had a hard time making up his mind.

After shoe shopping we went to Dairy Queen for a treat and then watched a play at an old playhouse on Main Street. The play wasn't very good, but they handed out marshmallows for us to throw at the villains.

I don't know how the play ended, because Jack kept throwing his marshmallows at the main girl and got himself kicked out.

Trevor and I decided to leave with him. The three of us and Seussol waited outside of the playhouse for everyone else to finish watching the play.

I was trying to use single words because now almost everything else I said was coming out as a rhyme. It was pretty embarrassing, and it made me want to help Seussol so he could return to the closet and I could start talking normal again instead of saying stuff that didn't make sense.

IF WE HAD A BUTTER BATTLE, I'D FLING BUTTER WITH A PADDLE. BUT IF WE HAD A WAFFLE WAR, IT'D BE TASTIER FOR SURE.

OR, WHAT IF WE DIDN'T FIGHT AND JUST HAD A NICE BREAKFAST TOMORROW?

When the play ended, everyone came out and we walked back to the hotel. My parents went to their room with Tuffin, Libby and Melany went to theirs, and me and my friends went to ours. There were two beds in our room and a roll-away cot. Me and Trevor got the beds, and Jack took the roll-away.

I LIKE MY BEDS TO HAVE WHEELS.

I made a little nest on the chair next to me for Seussol. He took off the ring and reappeared. He rested in the nest while we all stared at him and asked questions to all his personalities.

DO YOU KNOW-O ABOUT FRODO?

ARE ORCS AS SCARY AS THEY SEEM?

WHY HOP ON POP?

Seussol seemed to love our questions, and he answered them all using one of his three personalities.

After a ton of questions, Trevor began to yawn loudly and Jack put on his headphones and closed his eyes. Seussol got comfortable in his chair. He looked a little sad.

So I went to my parents' room and softly knocked on the door. My mom opened up and held her finger in front of her mouth to indicate that Tuffin was asleep and I needed to be quiet.

My mom got me the *book* and promised not to tell my dad even though I didn't ask her to. I read it to Seussol and then called it a night.

HI, IS IT-A-NIGHT THERE? YES, THIS IS ROB BURNSIDE CALLING IT-A-NIGHT.

CHAPTER 13

THE EPIC QUEST

I slept well and *so* did Seussol. In the morning, me
and my friends went down and took full advantage
of the free breakfast.

I felt like I needed to say that so they didn't think we were just three freeloaders trying to make off with sausage and waffles.

After breakfast my mom and Tuffin took a shuttle to the petting zoo, and Libby and Melany took one to the outlet mall. The trail to Bartholomew's Hat wasn't that far away from our hotel so we walked about half a mile to where the trail began.

At first it was kind of a nice hike. The ground was fairly level, and the trees and the grass and flowers swayed with the light wind. But after about two miles, the trail became steep, the trees looked mean, and the wind blew against us like a big bully. Seussol stayed on my shoulder the whole time. Occasionally he would whisper something in my ear like,

METHINKS MASTER ROBBIT IS BEGINNING TO SMELL OF SWEAT.

A little over halfway there, Seussol jumped off my shoulder to go chase what he thought was a wounded goblin. I just kept hiking and trying to look tougher than Trevor and Jack. Trevor was holding up, but Jack was complaining every step.

It's probably not smart to go on a long hike in new shoes, but there was no way my dad was going to just leave Jack in the woods while we kept going. I wanted to turn back too, but I knew this was a quest we had to finish. My dad tried to cheer Jack on.

While my dad was consulting the map, he noticed a shortcut that went through a long mining tunnel and came out near Bartholomew's Hat.

I whispered to see if Seussol was back on my shoulder yet. He didn't reply, and I had no idea if we needed to stick to the designated trail or if it was okay to take shortcuts on our quest. I tried to get everyone to stay on the trail, but Jack kept chanting,

I really wanted to take a shorter route too. I mean, it sounded fun to hike through a mining tunnel. But I needed to make sure Seussol could find us. My dad started walking again, and he broke off from the main trail and headed toward a cliff wall. We all followed. I pretended like I was singing some folksy song, but I was really just trying to call out for Seussol.

SEUSSOL, SEUSSOL, SEUSSOL, I HOPE YOU HEAR ME YELL! SEUSSOL, SEUSSOL, SEUSSOL, WE'RE HEADING OFF THE TRAIL!

THAT'S CATCHY!

Trevor joined in, and we sang all the way to the opening of the tunnel. I think the sign made us a little nervous about our choice. Jack tried to sound brave:

The tunnel was really dark. It wound through the mountain and smelled wet and salty. The flashlight didn't shine that far ahead, so we couldn't see much. My dad suddenly stopped and asked,

For the record, that's not a good thing for an adult to ask kids when they're in the middle of a dark tunnel in a strange part of the world. One of my friends started to whimper. I'm not sure which one because it was so dark. My dad said,

THERE'S SOMETHING MOVING BEHIND US.

My dad had just made both of my friends whimper. I would have joined in, but I was hoping that whatever was moving behind us was Seussol.

My dad offered an explanation, but my friends weren't buying it.

IT'S PROBABLY JUST THE WIND.

THE WIND DOESN'T MAKE FOOTSTEPS.

ARE YOU TRYING TO FREAK ME OUT?

I wanted to pretend that I wasn't scared, but when I put my hand on my chest, I could feel my heart beating wildly. I could also feel the manly necklace Janae had given me to remember her. It was hard to believe that not that long ago I was sitting with her in the safety of the Temon Mall eating fries and listening to her tell me about fascinating things like,

I hoped I wouldn't become one of those dying guys. We all started to walk faster through the tunnel. My dad kept saying that there was nothing to worry about, but then he added,

We all started to walk much faster. Actually, our walking had turned into a run. Jack took turns screaming for his safety and then screaming about his feet. Trevor was blowing his whistle as hard as he could, and my dad was hollering,

LIGHT UP AHEAD!!

I could see the end of the tunnel. Jack shoved us all aside to race for the light. Trevor kept blowing his whistle while my dad told us to panic in an orderly fashion. We busted out of the tunnel, and the light flooded our eyes. Nobody stopped running, because we still thought there could be a mountain lion behind us. But the light was blinding and our eyes had not adjusted to the sun yet.

Jack tripped over a tree root, and Trevor crashed into him. I fell over Trevor, and my dad tripped over another root and flew over all of us. We all came to a stop in a big heap at the base of a tree.

We looked back at the tunnel we had just passed through. There was nothing coming out. But as I stood up, I could feel something jump up onto my shoulder and grab hold of my neck.

The mining tunnel turned out to be a really good shortcut. I could see Bartholomew's Hat right in front of us now, sparkling under the sunlight.

I was excited to climb to the top. Jack was not. His feet really hurt, and he wasn't sure he could take another step.

There was really only one solution. It was weird, but it seemed promising, and my dad kept talking about how the solution was good for him too.

It was not easy climbing the stone stairs up to the top of Bartholomew's Hat. My dad had to set Jack down at least a dozen times. My legs were sore. Seussol wasn't tired at all.

When we finally reached the top, we were exhausted. I was surprised we had made it, surprised that my dad had not died carrying Jack, surprised that Trevor was still happy, and surprised to find that on top of Bartholomew's Hat there was a small gift shack next to a fire. It wasn't very exotic.

The biggest surprise was how Horton, the gift shack guy, reacted to seeing us. For some reason, Horton was excited about Jack. It was like he thought he was a king or something. Jack climbed down off of my dad's shoulders and proclaimed,

I COULD USE A RESTROOM.

Horton went on and on about how Jack was wearing a shirt with the face of Bartholomew. When

Horton saw the Beardy imprint on Jack's hand, he almost passed out.

Horton told us that many years ago, his grandfather made things out of metal from the area, and that he crafted a doorknob out of the best materials and with the special fire of Bartholomew. When Horton heard that I owned the doorknob, he turned to me and told me to . . .

I thought it was funny that Beardy's real name was Bartholomew. My dad was pretty confused by everything that was happening. He had been the one who had found Beardy at a garage sale and brought him home for my closet. And now some strange man on the top of a big hat-shaped rock was telling us that my doorknob was special.

THE FIRE ON THIS HILL HAS BURNED FOR HUNDREDS OF YEARS. THOSE THINGS CRAFTED IN THE FIRE HAVE A POWERFUL EFFECT. I'VE TRIED TO CARRY ON THE TRADITION, BUT I'M NOT QUITE AS TALENTED.

BARTHOLOMEW'S FIRE

While Horton was showing us his awful creations, out of the corner of my eye I could see that something was happening near the fire. Seussol had hopped from my shoulder and had slipped the ring off his finger. He was roasting one of his rings like a marshmallow.

I wanted to know what he was doing, but I also didn't want to give away Seussol's identity. Horton had gone nuts when he saw Jack's hand. I imagined he would freak out if he saw Seussol. My dad, as usual, was interested in everything and wanted to learn more from Horton, but he was also distracted. He needed to go back to the hotel and get ready for his speech, and he knew it would be slow going with Jack. I could feel Seussol jump back onto my shoulder.

I wasn't really sure what he had done, but I was glad he had done it. This quest had been almost as weird as I thought it would be. My dad told Horton all about the award he was going to win and how we needed to hurry off. So we left the top of Bartholomew's Hat and began the return hike. Unfortunately, the hike back to the hotel took forever. Nobody wanted to take the tunnel, so it was extra long, and Jack complained the whole way.

When we finally made it to the hotel, it was only an hour or so until my dad's award ceremony. My father practically threw Jack off his shoulders and raced to his room to get ready. Libby and Melany were in the lobby with my mom and Tuffin. Tuffin was pretty pumped up, because he had won a goldfish from one of the games at the petting zoo. My mom wasn't as pumped.

Seussol jumped from my shoulder. I couldn't see him, but it sounded like he was swinging from one of the hotel chandeliers. While Jack and Trevor were fighting over who would press the button on the elevator and my mom and Tuffin walked away, I looked at the chandelier and asked,

Seussol's three personalities were not easy to understand, but the cat part of him was right about the day being a very different-doofy-day.

CHAPTER 14

HOTEL ALONE

For some reason my parents decided that they didn't want to bring Tuffin to the awards ceremony.

WE ALSO THINK JACK COULD BE A PROBLEM.

So they were going to take Libby and Melany and wanted us to stay in our room and keep an eye on Tuffin. And as my mom put it,

DON'T TOUCH A SINGLE THING!

I was pretty happy about not going. I was tired from hiking, and room service and movies sounded great.

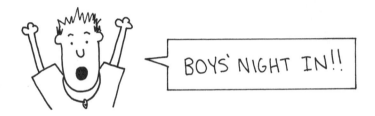

BOYS' NIGHT IN!!

After my parents left, we ordered a bunch of food and half a cake. I tried to get Seussol to appear so that he could tell us what had happened on Bartholomew's Hat. It took a lot of begging, but finally he slipped off the ring and materialized.

He told us how he had needed to take some of the rings to the fire and make something important. He pulled it out of his pocket and showed us.

We all looked closely at the strange object. It didn't look that amazing. Trevor asked about the other rings. Seussol told us that all the rings had numbers. The ones he had forged in the fire were rings three, four, five, and six. The one he was wearing was ring seven. Trevor wanted to see the others. Seussol reached into his pocket and pulled the remaining rings out. He laid them on the wood table.

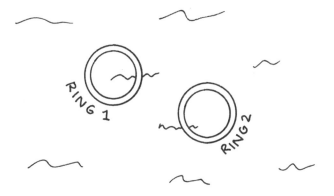

It was at that moment that room service knocked on the door and I went and opened it. They pushed a cart covered with food in and left. When I closed the door and looked back, I saw Jack and Tuffin

holding ring one and ring two.

Seussol should have known better than to tell

Jack and Tuffin what not to do. Of course they both

slipped the rings on.

I don't know how to explain it, but something happened to Jack and Tuffin. Their eyes went wild, and their hair puffed up. They started running around the room jumping on things.

STOP WHAT YOU'RE DOING.
STOP IT, I SAY!
TAKE THOSE RINGS OFF THIS INSTANT.
PUT BOTH RINGS AWAY!

This was bad. I was now in full rhyme mode, and Jack and Tuffin were in full mess mode.

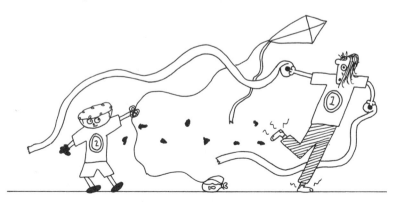

Ring One and Ring Two! They ran up, they ran through. They knocked down the lamps and the food they all threw. They smeared things on windows and counters and floors. They kicked at the tables, the couches, and doors. They pushed over Trevor, they plowed right through me, they pounded on walls like a drum symphony. They broke a big plate, bent a fork and a spoon. They screamed like an angry Scram-a-bam-boon.

AAAHHHHHHHH!!

WAAAHH!

SCRAM-A-BAM-BOON

They swung from the light, they swam through the beds. They banged up our elbows, our knees, and our heads. They couldn't be caught, no, we three couldn't catch them, so we set up a trap to outwit and outmatch them.

Luckily, the shower trap worked. They both went for the cake, and when they were in there, we closed the shower door and locked them in. Seussol hopped over the door and took off both the rings they had put on. Jack and Tuffin just stood in the shower looking confused.

We let them out and then all of us left the
bathroom and took a good look at the hotel room.
It was a mess. Actually, it was worse than a mess.

I explained to Jack that he and Tuffin had done it. I also explained that if we didn't get it cleaned up, we were going to be in big trouble. My mom had said not to mess up anything, and here we had messed up everything.

HAVE NO FEAR, MY DEAR ROB, WE WILL CLEAN DOWN AND UP, WITH THIS WONDERFUL, FABULOUS, FOOD-CARTY CART.

Seussol pushed the cart around the room and began cleaning and scrubbing with supplies from the closet. His energy was more contagious than my aunt Sally's swamp fever. Everyone began to pick up and clean. We put all the messy things on the cart

and worked as a team, scrubbing the walls and
putting things in order.

It took us a long time, but when we were done, I
pushed the cart out into the hall and down in front
of the maids' station. It looked a little different than
when it was first dropped off with our food on it.

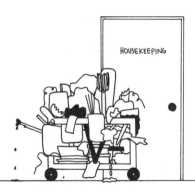

Ten minutes after I got back to the room, my parents returned with Libby and Melany. My dad wanted to show us his award, so he came into our room. He was so excited he didn't even notice that our blankets and sheets were missing or that a few things had been rearranged.

THIS IS THE OUTIE AWARD. OUTIE STANDS FOR OUTSTANDING! NO OTHER PLAYGROUND SALESMAN HAS EVER WON ONE OF THESE.

WOW!

WOW IS RIGHT. I'D BETTER GO LIE DOWN.

When my dad left, we all sighed a sigh of relief. Seussol appeared and started talking about how he wanted to take a bath to unwind. So I drew him a bath and let him unwind.

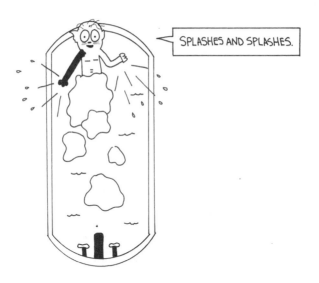

After he finished his bath, I wrapped Seussol in a blanket and read him a book to help put him to sleep. Trevor and Jack listened in.

I felt the same way about them.

CHAPTER 15

SICK

The next morning, we checked out of the hotel and took the train back down the mountains. As we got onto the train, Jack asked:

DOES THE TRAIN GO FASTER WHEN IT'S GOING DOWNHILL? I HOPE SO. TELL THEM NOT TO USE THEIR BRAKES.

Actually the train did go a lot faster on the ride down. Me and Seussol spent some time at the back of the train watching the mountains disappear. I wasn't certain, but I thought I could *see* the fire on top of Bartholomew's Hat.

We all ate lunch in the dining car, and *before* we knew it, the ride was over. We walked back to our RV and started the long drive home. We were taking a different way home. As my dad put it...

We stopped in a town called Thidwick, New Mexico, and parked for the night. We ate dinner at a restaurant shaped like a boat.

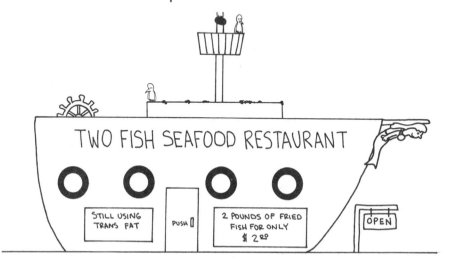

The food was greasy and delicious. We ate tons of it. I even fed some to Seussol under the table.

FISHES AND FISHES.

We probably shouldn't have eaten there. That night we all began to get horribly sick. It started with Libby.

The trip home was a blur. Everyone was ill. My father could barely drive, and the rest of us were sweating and throwing up. I know we drove the next day and parked somewhere, but I couldn't tell you where. Plus, Seussol was a mess.

I couldn't *see* straight, stand straight, or sleep straight.

When we finally arrived home, everyone stumbled out of the RV like characters from *The Walking Dead.*

I went straight to my room to lie down and maybe vomit. I closed my door and Seussol appeared. He looked worse than ever.

Seussol was so sick he was ready to go back into the closet.

Seussol reached into his pocket and pulled out the small metal object he had shown me in the hotel.

He explained that if I used the object on Beardy, it would let me know when the next time my closet was going to send a visitor.

Seussol took off his hat and dumped it on the floor. There were all kinds of objects. In fact, I think Seussol might have been the Temon Taker. I could see Wonk's cane and one of the garden gnomes from Trevor's front yard. Most surprising was when Jim flew out.

I opened my window, and Jim flew out, cursing Seussol. While I was turning around, I heard Beardy click open.

Seussol handed me ring number seven. I had been given some cool things by my past guests, but the ring was definitely my favorite.

And with that, Seussol was gone. The closet door closed and snapped. I tried to open it, but Beardy was locked tight. I took the weird object that Suessol had made in the fire. I pushed it up against the four corners of Beardy's head and it clicked.

Then I turned it slightly, and the front of the doorknob swung open like a pocket watch. There, behind it, was a date.

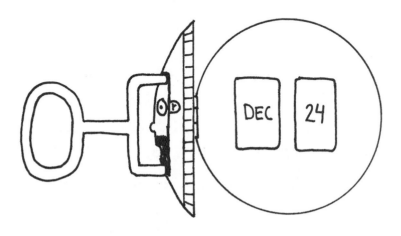

If this date meant what I thought it did, I had over a month before my next guest would arrive. I hoped I would feel better by then.

CHAPTER 16

MUCH BETTER

I actually got better a couple of days later. It was nice to be back home. It also helped that Janae brought me a get-well basket. I told her all about my trip, leaving out the parts about Seussol and everyone throwing up. But I wanted her to know that I was close to death because she had told me she liked books where the boy died.

I WANTED TO DIE.

WELL, I'M GLAD YOU DIDN'T.

My other friends came over and tried to make me feel as bad as possible about getting sick.

When Trevor got better, he edited all his film into a movie and showed it to everyone at his house.

It wasn't at all epic. It was actually really awful. The editing didn't make sense, and the story fell apart after about a minute. The only part I liked was the one scene where I could see a bit of Seussol.

I DECLARE THIS ADVENTURE TO BE... MIGHTY COOL!

Now that Seussol was gone, I no longer had the urge to rhyme. I was okay with that, but I missed having him hang out on my shoulder. Sometimes I would just pretend he was there.

HI, SEUSSOL.

HI, MASTER ROBBIT.

I liked knowing when a new creature was coming. It allowed me to enjoy a little calm before the next storm. I have been reading the Lord of the Rings. I finished *The Fellowship of the Ring,* and I'm currently halfway through *The Two Towers.* I can't believe how good the books are. I also can't believe that I don't want them to end. I suppose there's no such thing as a book that's too long, if the characters are great and the plot is so strong.

A few days ago, I was sitting in front of the window in the family room when my mom came in from getting the mail.

She had a question for me. She had just received a letter from the Grand Hotel claiming that we owed them for a couple of broken plates, a bent fork, and a cracked lamp they found on a beat-up food cart. She wanted to know if I knew anything about it.

Should I tell her about it?

Now, what should I do?

Well . . . what would you do

if my mother asked you?

COMING SOON

GOD BUILD US.
EVERY BRICK.

BATNEEZER

THE CREATURE
FROM MY CLOSET

Book 6

MAE
ROB